# Naughty Nautical Neighbors

Patrick dipped his bubble wand, whispered a message into a new bubble, and sent it SpongeBob's way. When it popped, he heard: "Hey, SpongeBob!"

"Tee-hee-hee!" SpongeBob laughed.

Squidward sighed. "How did I ever get surrounded by such loser neighbors?"

Then it was SpongeBob's turn again. He took a deep breath and exhaled a whisper into a bubble: "Patrick, you're my best friend in the whole neighborhood."

"Aarrgghh!" Squidward couldn't take it anymore. "I must figure out how to shut those two up!" An evil plan quickly formed in his squishy head. He went over to his soufflé and drained some of the liquid out and into a cup. He stirred it vigorously until it began to foam up. Then he, too, blew a message into a bubble and sent it out his window toward Patrick.

Squidward's bubble caught up with another bubble that was already making its way toward Patrick. It was a bubble showdown!

*Stephen Hillenburg*

Based on the TV series *SpongeBob SquarePants*®
created by Stephen Hillenburg as seen on Nickelodeon®

ISBN 0-439-34147-7

12 11 10 9 8 7 6 5 4 3 2 1          1 2 3 4 5 6/0

Printed in the U.S.A.

First Scholastic printing, September 2001

# Naughty Nautical Neighbors

by **Annie Auerbach**
illustrated by **Mark O'Hare**
based on an original teleplay by
**Sherm Cohen, Aaron Springer,**
**and Mr. Lawrence**

SCHOLASTIC INC.
New York  Toronto  London  Auckland  Sydney
Mexico City  New Delhi  Hong Kong  Buenos Aires

# chapter one

Deep in the Pacific Ocean, way below the tropical isle of Bikini Atoll, lies the underwater city of Bikini Bottom. It isn't on any map because no one could possibly chart a place like Bikini Bottom! In this underwater paradise, fish walk, clams talk, and the Krusty Krab—home of the Krabby Patty—is just down the block.

Bikini Bottom is also the home of Squidward Tentacles. Just about everything annoys this whiny and bitter squid. If Squidward had his way, he would be left alone to play his beloved clarinet and work on his gallery of self-portraits.

On one particular day, Squidward was cooking up a simply spectacular dish.

"Woooooow!" Squidward exclaimed, admiring his work. "This is the best soufflé I've ever created!"

The soufflé was in the shape of a little mountain. On top sat a miniature version of Squidward, sitting on a throne under a little palm tree. He looked like the king of the world—or at least the king of *his* little world.

Squidward tasted his culinary creation. "Mmmmm . . . congratulations, Chef! You're a genius!" he declared. "But, wait! A dish like this calls for my best eating attire."

Quickly, Squidward threw off his apron. He

jumped into a bath and started scrubbing.

*"I am the greatest chef on the ocean floor,"* he sang at the top of his lungs. *"There's no one better than me!"*

When he was squeaky clean, Squidward hopped out of the bath, grabbed a towel, and dried around each of his numerous suction cups. Finally, he put on his best pressed suit.

"Well, I look stunning, if I do say so myself," he said. "And I do!" Then, licking his chops, he added, "And now . . . it's time to eat!"

Sitting down at the table, he picked up a knife and fork. Squidward was about to dig in when he heard a familiar sound. A sound that would make his hair stand up—if he had any. A sound that annoyed him twenty-four hours a day . . . the sound of SpongeBob SquarePants!

"Tee-hee-hee!" came from outside Squidward's window.

"Oh, no!" Squidward groaned.

"Tee-hee-hee!" was heard again.

Squidward stood up and went to the window to see his nightmare come true: There sat SpongeBob SquarePants with his best friend, Patrick Star. All three of these nautical neighbors lived next door to each other in this area of Bikini Bottom.

"There goes my peace and quiet!" complained Squidward.

SpongeBob and Patrick were sitting on opposite sides of Squidward's pathway, playing a game. They each had a bottle of bubbles and a bubble wand. One would whisper into a bubble, and the bubble would then float over to the other friend and "pop" out a message. It was their favorite game.

SpongeBob dipped his bubble wand. Then he whispered into it and sent it off toward

Patrick. When the bubble reached him, it popped and said: "Hi, Patrick."

"Tee-hee-hee!" giggled Patrick.

Squidward didn't find this funny at all. To him it was just *extremely* annoying.

Patrick dipped his bubble wand, whispered a message into a new bubble, and sent it SpongeBob's way. When it popped, he heard: "Hey, SpongeBob!"

"Tee-hee-hee!" SpongeBob laughed.

Squidward sighed. "How did I ever get surrounded by such loser neighbors?"

Then it was SpongeBob's turn again. He took a deep breath and exhaled a whisper into a bubble: "Patrick, you're my best friend in the whole neighborhood."

"Aarrgghh!" Squidward couldn't take it anymore. "I must figure out how to shut those two up!" An evil plan quickly formed in his squishy head. He went over to his soufflé and drained some of the liquid out and into a cup. He stirred it vigorously until it began to foam up. Then he, too, blew a message into a bubble and sent it out his window toward Patrick.

Squidward's bubble caught up with another bubble that was already making its way toward Patrick. It was a bubble showdown! But Squidward's evil bubble soon kicked the other bubble into the deep blue sea, never to be heard from again.

The "evil" bubble popped near Patrick's ear. It was Squidward imitating SpongeBob: "Patrick, you are the dumbest idiot it has ever been my misfortune to know."

"What?" said Patrick. He immediately whispered a message into another bubble and sent it to SpongeBob: "Do you really think that, SpongeBob?"

Of course, SpongeBob knew nothing about Squidward's dirty tricks. He didn't know that Squidward was imitating him and calling Patrick an idiot. He didn't know that his message about Patrick being his best friend was being replaced with Squidward's mean one.

So, in his good-natured way, SpongeBob sent a bubble to Patrick that said, "Of course, Patrick! Anyone with eyes could see that!"

Patrick was shocked. "That's it!" he declared, and blew into another bubble. "Well, I think you're ugly! And . . . and . . . yellow is ugly!"

"Patrick, what are you talking about?!" asked a very confused SpongeBob. Then Squidward decided it was time to stir up even more trouble. He immediately made more and more bubbles to send out. Imitating Patrick,

Squidward whispered into a few bubbles and sent them in SpongeBob's direction. The first one popped: "SpongeBob, I no longer wish to know you."

SpongeBob couldn't believe what he was hearing!

Then another bubble popped in front of SpongeBob: "You give bottom dwellers a bad name!"

"WHAT?!" cried SpongeBob.

And another bubble popped: "If I had a dollar for every brain you don't have, I'd have ONE dollar!"

Squidward couldn't help snickering at his own insults. "This is the perfect revenge to get back at those two!"

Then, imitating SpongeBob, Squidward whispered into a bubble and sent it to Patrick: "Hey, Patrick, I heard there was a job opening down at the pet shop—as some NEWSPAPER!"

"Well, you're a big dummy, you DUMMY!" yelled Patrick.

SpongeBob narrowed his eyes. "Yeah? Well, that means that . . . so are you!" he yelled back.

"Uh . . . dummy!" Patrick shouted.

"Sticks and stones make clog my pores, but names will never hurt me!" replied SpongeBob, his hands on his hips.

As SpongeBob and Patrick continued to argue and call each other names, Squidward took a lawn chair outside. He planted himself ringside, with his soufflé and a fork. "There's nothing better than dinner theater!" He laughed.

"And you're a turkey!" continued Patrick.

"Well, you're a bigger one!" SpongeBob shot back.

Patrick had to think fast. "Well, you're *still* yellow and you know what else is yellow?"

"What?" said SpongeBob.

"YOU ARE!" replied Patrick.

"Oh, good one!" Squidward said with a nod.

SpongeBob couldn't take it anymore. He yelled at Patrick, "Yeah? Well, it doesn't matter what you call me, because I never want to see you again, anyway!"

"I don't want to see you, either!" Patrick replied, and stormed off to his house.

SpongeBob rushed into his own house. "Aw, tartar sauce!" he said, slamming the door.

# chapter two

"Ha-ha-ha-ha-ha!" cackled Squidward.

Squidward was laughing so hard, he didn't realize there was still a forkful of food in his mouth. "Ha-ha-ha-ha-ha . . . gulp . . . ccckkkk!" Suddenly he began to choke! Not only was he choking on his soufflé, but on the fork, too!

He tried to swallow. "Gguauu—"

Patrick peeked out from his house and ran outside. "Wow, Squidward, you're choking!" Patrick pointed out.

Squidward just glared at him.

"I know what to do, but I should wash my hands first," Patrick said.

But by this time, Squidward was looking worse. He was turning an even uglier shade of greenish gray.

"Oh, well!" Patrick said, and took a deep breath. He put his mouth over Squidward's and exhaled. The more air Patrick blew into Squidward's mouth, the more Squidward's body began to inflate. Patrick hoped all the air would dislodge the fork. But instead, Squidward's body blew up like a balloon—even the suction cups on all of his arms popped!

Finally, Squidward let out a big breath, and the fork came flying out! It landed right in Patrick's hands.

"Oooh! It worked!" Patrick said, quite pleased with himself.

Thankful to be alive, Squidward gushed, "Wow! Patrick you *saved* me!"

"I did?!" Patrick said.

"Yep!" Squidward declared. "You're a real lifesaver, friend!"

"Friend?" Patrick repeated. "Ooh . . . friend."

Squidward nodded. "Yeah, Patrick," he said casually. "We're friends."

But "friend" was a magic word to Patrick. Now that SpongeBob was out of the picture, Patrick had plenty of time to spend with his *new* friend. "So, what are we doing tonight, best friend?" he asked Squidward enthusiastically.

"Well, I was going to practice my clarinet SOLO," answered Squidward.

"Great! Let's go!" Patrick said, putting an arm around Squidward.

Uh-oh. What have I done? Squidward thought as they went inside.

# chapter three

Being next-door neighbors, SpongeBob had easily overheard Patrick and Squidward's conversation. He heard that Patrick *already* had a new best friend.

"Aw . . . who needs 'em!" SpongeBob said firmly. He looked around his home. It was a fully furnished, two-bedroom pineapple. "They're no fun, anyway, right, Gary? Gary?"

Gary, SpongeBob's pet snail, seemed to be busy deep inside his shell at the moment.

"What am I worried about?" SpongeBob said to himself. "I've got plenty of other friends." He looked around and then picked up a pen and drew faces on three of his fingers. "I could name three right off the bat!"

SpongeBob wiggled his fingers. He sighed and said weakly, "Woo-hoo! The gang's all here." Then he began to sob. "I have no friends at all! Patrick's a deserter, and even Gary's too busy for me!"

Suddenly SpongeBob heard Squidward next door. He jumped up and ran to the window to see what was going on.

"Tonight I will be performing my version of Solitude in E Minor," Squidward said.

"E Minor. All right!" cheered Patrick. "Yeah, yeah!"

Squidward just ignored Patrick. Then he took a deep breath and played only one note before he heard, "ZZZZZZZZzzzzzzz."

Patrick had fallen asleep.

"Oh, puh-leeze!" Squidward groaned. "Patrick, wake up! Wake up, you lazy invertebrate!"

SpongeBob giggled as he watched from his window. He knew Patrick wouldn't wake up for anything!

"That's it!" cried Squidward. "I can't play with that annoying racket!" Then he put down his clarinet and went over to the snoring starfish. Yelling at him didn't work. Shaking him didn't work. Even tickling him didn't work. "Oh, why me?" moaned Squidward. "Why me?!"

Finally, Squidward put his arms under Patrick's arms and began to drag him out the front door. "Grr-grunt-grunt!" Squidward groaned.

When he eventually got Patrick outside, Squidward suddenly screeched, "OH! My back! I threw out my back!"

"Oh, boy!" exclaimed SpongeBob, who was still watching from his window. "Now's my chance!"

SpongeBob raced outside. He took a running start and then bounced off his diving board. SpongeBob sailed through the water. Before Squidward knew it, SpongeBob was zooming right at him!

Squidward looked up in horror. "SpongeBob—no!" he shrieked. "Stay back!"

"Hang on!" SpongeBob called, his speed increasing.

"Stay away from me!" Squidward warned.

But SpongeBob was a sponge with a mission. "I'll save you!" he yelled, closing in.

"NO!" Squidward cried. He desperately

tried to get back inside his house. But since he had thrown out his back, he couldn't run away from SpongeBob. He couldn't run at all. In fact, he could barely walk.

Just as Squidward made it back to his front door, SpongeBob plowed right into his back.

"AAARRGGGHHH!" Squidward yelled in pain. "I'm ruined!" Then he moved around a bit and was surprised to find that he actually felt better! "Hey, I feel great! Thanks, SpongeBob, you're a real friend."

SpongeBob's eyes glazed over, and his smile grew. "Fr-iend?" he repeated.

Realizing his mistake, Squidward quickly said, "Uh . . . no! I didn't mean—"

"Don't worry about it, Squiddy, ol' pal!" said SpongeBob. "That's what friends are for."

"Oh, great, *another* friend," said Squidward. "Here we go again. . . ."

# chapter four

As Squidward went inside his house, he found that SpongeBob was *right* behind him.

"So, dumb Patrick fell asleep on you, huh?" SpongeBob asked.

"Uh-huh," replied Squidward.

"Some friend he is!" said SpongeBob. "A real friend would perform for *you!*"

Suddenly, Squidward perked up. "Do you play?" he asked excitedly.

"Are you kidding?" SpongeBob said,

quickly looking around. "I've been playing the bassinet for years!" SpongeBob lied, grabbing the bass nearby. "Give me an A, buddy!"

Squidward played an A on his clarinet.

SpongeBob took the bow and *tried* to play. The noise he was making was painful. To make matters worse, he began to sing off-key: *"Squidward is my best friend in the world! Squidward is my best friend in the sea!"*

The combination of horrific sounds made Squidward drop his clarinet. "AHHH!" he shouted, cringing.

But SpongeBob kept playing and singing: *"I'm Squidward's very best friend. He doesn't like anyone more than me!"*

SpongeBob was playing the bass with so much gusto that the bow actually got caught and pulled back like an archer's arrow. The bow went flying—and straight into Squidward—a

*painting* of Squidward, that is. Squidward loved to re-create himself—be it as paintings, wax models, or on the tops of soufflés.

Squidward went over to the painting, angrily pulled out the bow, and broke it in two. "SpongeBob!" he yelled.

SpongeBob just continued. He began to strum the bass like a guitar, instead, singing, *"Squidward—"*

*". . . likes Patrick more than SpongeBob!"* Patrick chimed in.

SpongeBob whirled around to see Patrick sticking his head through the window. SpongeBob stomped over to it and slammed the window shut. Then he picked up the bass and slammed it on the ground with every word: *"And Patrick is a dirty, stinky, rotten friend stealer!"*

The bass was now in pieces. "Um . . . I can fix this," SpongeBob said, embarrassed.

Squidward's face turned red with anger. His squid blood was beginning to boil!

"Squidward?" SpongeBob said nervously. "Squiddy? Pal? Friend? Buddy? Amigo?"

With one swift kick from Squidward, SpongeBob found himself outside. He picked himself up and uneasily yelled to Squidward, "So, uh . . . I'll see you later? Uh . . . call me!"

# chapter five

"ICK!" cried Squidward. "That was disgusting. I feel like I need to scrub myself. Maybe I can wash away all that gross 'friendship' talk." He sighed and headed into the bathroom.

"AAAHH!" Squidward shouted suddenly.

Patrick was back—and in the tub! "Hey, *buddy,* I warmed it up for you!" Patrick said. He was holding a bar of soap and a scrub brush.

Squidward had had it! "Patrick, get out!" he

demanded. "And put some clothes on!"

Just then SpongeBob poked his head in through the bathroom window. "I thought I heard some . . . aha! So *this* is what I find, huh? My best friend and my *ex*-best friend! And . . . and . . . rubber bath toys!"

"Oh, yeah? Well, he was my friend first!" Patrick stated.

SpongeBob wasn't about to back down. "Patrick, you're just a backbiting, bathtub-filling, blob of—"

Patrick cut him off. "I'm rubber, you're glue, whatever you say bounces off me and sticks to you!"

"Oh, that's really original," SpongeBob said in a snotty voice. "Besides, you're such a big blob that *everything* bounces off you!"

Squidward looked at the two of them arguing back and forth. He turned and ran out of the bathroom and the house, screaming, "This can't be happening to me!" He hid in a garbage can outside.

Back inside, SpongeBob and Patrick stopped their name-calling long enough to realize that Squidward was no longer there.

"Squidward?" called SpongeBob.

"Hey, Squidward!" Patrick said. "Buddy?"

But there was no way Squidward was going back in the house with his two new "friends."

This is nuts! Squidward thought to himself, still inside the garbage can. Those two are making my life miserable! I need a plan to get them back together and out of my way!

# chapter six

The next day, SpongeBob was reading *A Tale of Two Squiddies* when the doorbell rang. An envelope was slipped under his front door.

"What's this?" SpongeBob wondered aloud as he picked it up and smelled it. "Aaaahh . . . Squidward." He tore open the envelope. "A dinner party? Tonight? Thrown by Squidward? I'd love to!" he exclaimed.

Later that day, after a long bath, SpongeBob ran into his bedroom and opened up the closet.

"What to wear, what to wear . . . ," he pondered.

Finally, after careful consideration, SpongeBob chose a white shirt, a red tie, a pair of brown, square pants, and a pair of black shoes. "Perfect," he said as he looked in the mirror. "I'm ready!"

"Squidward!" called SpongeBob as he knocked on his next-door neighbor's door. "Oh, Squidward-iard!"

Inside, Squidward groaned. "Let's get this over with," he said to himself, and opened the door.

"Did you miss me?" SpongeBob asked with a grin.

"Come on in!" Squidward replied cheerfully. "You look stunning!"

SpongeBob beamed. "Gee, thanks! I'd

much rather dine with *you* than that lousy . . . EEK!"

SpongeBob looked across the room to see his ex-best friend, Patrick, sitting at the table!

"Say, what gives? I'm not sitting near that maniac!" insisted SpongeBob.

"Me either!" Patrick added. "This was a setup!"

"But I thought you two were my best friends," Squidward said innocently.

"I *am* your best friend!" SpongeBob quickly said.

"No, *I* am!" Patrick declared.

"I am!" countered SpongeBob.

"Enough!" Squidward screamed. Then, remembering his master plan, he sweetly said, "How about some appetizers, guys?"

Patrick's stomach growled.

"I'll take that as a 'yes,'" said Squidward.

"Be right back," he added, and headed into the kitchen to begin Plan A. . . .

SpongeBob reluctantly took a seat at the table. Immediately, he and Patrick had their backs to each other. Neither one was going to be the first to talk. It was silent for a few minutes, with the only noise coming from Patrick's stomach. The tension in the room was worse than a sea of hungry anchovies.

Luckily, Squidward came back from the kitchen. "Who wants some delicious Krabby Patties?" he asked, holding a plateful of mini burgers.

"Oh! Me! Me!" SpongeBob and Patrick shouted at once. They each greedily grabbed a Krabby Patty off the plate.

"Now, now," Squidward began, "remember your manners. We're all friends here, right?"

SpongeBob put down the Krabby Patty he

was holding. "I'm not friends with *him*," he said, pointing to Patrick.

Patrick grabbed SpongeBob's Krabby Patty and swallowed it whole. "And I'm not friends with you, either," Patrick told SpongeBob.

"Then how come you ate my Krabby Patty?" asked SpongeBob.

"I was hungry," Patrick explained.

Suddenly it was a mad dash for the Krabby Patties. SpongeBob grabbed a bunch of Krabby Patties in his arms while Patrick grabbed a bunch in his mouth.

Squidward looked at the now empty plate he was holding. He didn't even get to eat one Krabby Patty. He trudged back into the kitchen. "All right, Plan A didn't work, so I guess it's time for Plan B."

# chapter seven

Squidward returned to the table with an old-fashioned soda bottle. "How about some soda?" he asked.

"Oh, yes, please!" answered SpongeBob. He held out a cup. "Thanks, *friend! Sluuurrp!*"

"How about some for your best friend?" Patrick asked Squidward, and held out his cup.

But SpongeBob was sneaky and put his own cup under the nozzle first. "Thanks, best friend! *Glug, glug, glug!*"

Patrick looked at Squidward and pleaded, "Can I have some now, buddy?"

"Wait! I need some more!" SpongeBob demanded.

"I still didn't get any!" Patrick said angrily.

SpongeBob took the few drops he had left in his cup and poured it into Patrick's. "There you go!" he said. Then he looked at Squidward and added, "More, please!"

*Glug, glug, glug.*

"More, Squidward!" said Patrick.

*Glug, glug, glug.*

"More, Squidward!" said SpongeBob.

*Glug, glug, glug.*

"More, Squidward!" called Patrick.

*Glug, glug, glug.*

"More, Squidward!" called SpongeBob.

*Glug, glug, glug.*

"Squidward!"

"Squidward!"

SpongeBob and Patrick went through one cup of soda after another. Squidward could hardly keep up with them. It seemed that every time he filled one's cup, the other one's was empty.

"Sorry, boys, I'm all out of soda," Squidward finally said. "I'm going to get some more. Why don't you two just stay here and chat?" he said with a sneaky smile, and quickly left.

By this time, SpongeBob and Patrick were so full of soda that they looked like two huge balloons.

"Hiccup!" said SpongeBob.

Patrick tried his hardest not to laugh out loud.

"Hiccup!" repeated SpongeBob.

"Burp!" went Patrick.

SpongeBob couldn't help but giggle.

Patrick couldn't keep it in, either!

All this burping and hiccuping started to make them laugh. And once they started laughing, there was no stopping them. Soon bubbles filled the whole room, and they both started to lift up into the air. They became lighter as they burped out all the gas from the soda.

SpongeBob and Patrick were having so much fun, they forgot why they had even started arguing in the first place.

As the two friends floated in the air, the bubbles kept multiplying. They filled the entire house. Soon the house became *too* full of bubbles. The house began to shake. It was ready to burst!

Just then, Squidward returned home with more soda. He was about to put his key in the door when—*KABOOM!* Squidward's house exploded!

I should just walk away right now, Squidward told himself. He took a deep breath and fearfully opened the door. Once the bubbles cleared, Squidward looked around at what once was his house. Now it was mostly rubble; no walls were left, not to mention any of the furniture or paintings. The only thing left intact was the door.

Squidward sighed. "What a surprise. I invited them in, and I left them alone. Well, Squidward, what have we learned, today?" He glared at SpongeBob and Patrick, who were standing there, looking innocent.

"Guess what, Squidward?" SpongeBob said excitedly.

"Oh, this should be good . . . ," mumbled Squidward.

Patrick piped up. "Me and SpongeBob are friends again!"

"Great. Go be friends somewhere else," replied Squidward through his teeth.

"Don't you want us to help you clean this up a little?" asked SpongeBob.

"NO! OUT!" Squidward shouted.

SpongeBob and Patrick quickly made their way out past Squidward.

"Psst!" SpongeBob whispered to Patrick. "I think he's jealous."

"How pathetic," Patrick whispered. "Come on. Let's get our bottles of bubbles!"

Squidward slammed the door once they left. A leftover bubble floated by and popped when it hit the door.

*BAM!*

The door fell over—and right on top of Squidward. "Oh! My back!" he cried. "I'll get you, SpongeBob—once I can move!"

Once again, SpongeBob SquarePants had ruined everything of Squidward's—his back, his house, and especially his day!

Welcome to the sea. Beautiful, mysterious . . . and wet.

It is here where the dolphin frolics and the electric eel slithers. Where the shy octopus plays and the sea horse rides. But go farther down . . . all the way to the bottom of the ocean. Here is a world entirely different from what we know on dry land.

A strange world with different rules, funny customs . . . and unusual creatures.

"Wow! Four stingers!" a squeaky voice exclaimed as an angry jellyfish buzzed by. "Buzz away, jellyfish," the yellow box-shaped character continued in his best dramatic voice. "For soon you shall belong to . . . *SpongeBob SquarePants!*"

SpongeBob gave a few practice swings with his net in preparation to capture his prey.

Then, he readied himself as the jellyfish came around for another pass.

"Buzzzzzzzzzz," said the jellyfish.

SpongeBob buzzed back in his best jellyfish impersonation to lure him into his trap. "Steady," he whispered, readying his net. "Steady . . ."

The jellyfish slowed down and hovered over a blue sea anemone.

"Yes!" SpongeBob screeched, bounding out of hiding and bringing down his net.

The jellyfish avoided the attack and swam to the left.

SpongeBob followed suit, swinging the net in a sideways arc . . . but somehow caught himself instead!

Hanging in his own net, SpongeBob

watched sadly as the jellyfish zipped home to Jellyfish Fields.

Disappointed, SpongeBob continued to look for other jellyfish, but none were to be found. However, he did notice a funny-looking creature in a space suit wrestling a giant clam. . . .

SpongeBob did a double take. Space suit!? Could it be . . . space aliens?

He wiggled out of his net and ran toward the scene.

Upon closer inspection, SpongeBob saw that the space suit was actually a white high-tech diving suit. As for the clam . . . well, it was huge! And mean!

The spry fighter growled like a grizzly bear and used a combination of judo and karate—plus some moves SpongeBob had never even seen before—to fight the threatening clam.

The creature in a space helmet gave a final cry of triumph and conked the gray shell of the giant clam. It was this move that allowed SpongeBob to clearly see the fighter's face for the first time.

Where have I seen this before? SpongeBob wondered. Reaching into his pocket, he took out his handy *Barks Junior Field Guide.*

SpongeBob frantically flipped through the pages. "Ah-ha!" he cried, finding a page with a picture of the being in the diving suit. However, in the field guide, a furry head was exposed.

"Land squirrel," SpongeBob read aloud. "She's a land squirrel . . . whatever *that* is."

Suddenly, the squirrel gave out a loud grunt of surprise as the clam bit her leg.

"That little squirrel is in trouble!" SpongeBob announced. "This looks like a job for . . . SpongeBob!"

# about the author

For **Annie Auerbach**, it's been a wild ride from a background in theater and film to a career in publishing. Besides being an editor for a Los Angeles publishing company, she is also a freelance writer and the author of books based on Nickelodeon's *CatDog*, Disney's *A Bug's Life*, and many more. She's now grateful that her parents limited her TV viewing time as a kid—telling her to read a book instead!